Contents

Characters

Earthlings

Scott

Thirteen-year-old Scott's favourite things are science and skateboarding – and avoiding his snoopy big sister.

AJ

Scott's daredevil friend AJ is always taking crazy risks, and he has lots of cuts and bruises to show for it.

Rudy

The conscience of the group. He likes woodwork, hanging with Scott and AJ, and his Red Sox cap.

Penny

Scott's fourteen-year-old sister Penny likes to poke her nose into his life – and get him into trouble.

Halycrusians

Inhabitants of the environmentally ravaged planet Halycrus. They live underground, hiding from the vicious mountain swine.

Z-kee

T-kwinia

R-cher

PORTAL TO HALYCRUS

by Keira Wong

illustrated by Douglas Fong

SCHOLASTIC

This 2009 edition published in the United Kingdom by
Scholastic Ltd
Villiers House
Clarendon Avenue
Leamington Spa

Out of this World: Portal to Halycrus
ISBN 978 1407 10106 4

Printed by Tien Wah Press, Singapore

1 2 3 4 5 6 7 8 9   9 0 1 2 3 4 5 6 7 8

chapter 1

S u c k e d I n

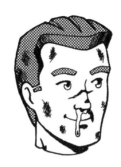

"Are you picking your nose?"

It's not something you want to admit to, even if your fingers are stained green. And especially if the person asking the question is your fussy and dramatic older sister.

"MUM!! Scott's picking his nose!"

I quickly tried to wipe the green stains away on my jeans.

"Yuck! He's wiping the bogeys on his clothes!"

Seven people with disgusted looks on their faces crammed into my bedroom.

"I'm not picking my nose. I'm doing my science project. I'm trying to show what happens when a virus attacks."

"So how come your fingers are green?" asked Penny.

I pointed to the shop mannequin beside me. "I'm shoving green slime up the mannequin's nose. It's made of borax, glue and water. And, um, er…" I trailed off. There was something I didn't want Penny to know. "It's supposed to imitate a cold," I mumbled.

Penny narrowed her eyes. "Why is it so pearly? Oh no, that's my Lime Ice eyeshadow! Mum, he's used my best eyeshadow to make fake snot!"

"Oh well, dear," Mum sighed. "Scott, just don't put that stuff anywhere near your mouth. Borax will poison you."

"I wish!" yelled Penny. She ran off in a huff. My brothers turned away, bored with the commotion.

My family usually doesn't pay much attention to me. But catch me with "snot" on my finger – in the name of science, of course – and they're all ears and boggling eyes. I normally slip by unnoticed. Like the time when my dad's courier service had an extra delivery of those bendy foam "noodles" that float in swimming pools. Nobody noticed when my best friends, Rudy and AJ, and I made a three-man toboggan to slide off the roof. Even when Rudy and I crashed into Mum's rose bush and AJ landed face first in the dog's dinner. It wasn't until AJ chased

Penny around the garden with dog food in his hand that we got any attention.

Normally, the only attention I get is when my family marvel about how different I look from the rest of them. They all have sandy blond hair and dark brown eyes. Me? Well, I have black hair and black eyes. I am literally the "black sheep" of the family. I don't mind. If my family paid attention to me, they would have foiled our noodle/toboggan creation before it ever got on to the roof. And that would have been a shame.

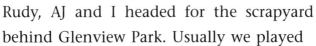

Mum and Dad

Penny
14 years old.

Dean
9 years old.

Ryan
9 years old.

✪ ✪ ✪

Rudy, AJ and I headed for the scrapyard behind Glenview Park. Usually we played video games after school, but today AJ had decided we should check out the yard for old bike parts. AJ was behind most of our ideas.

Trouble was, the scrapyard was in the opposite direction to

Bella
6 months old.

Olly
4 years old.

home. I was stuck carrying my snot science project with me.

"Look at you, carrying a doll," Rudy chuckled softly, tipping back his Red Sox cap.

"It's not a doll. It's a mannequin for my science project," I said. "See, I carved out the nostrils and put fake snot up there."

"Are you sure it's fake?" asked AJ, sneaking up behind us and pulling Rudy's cap over his eyes. He flashed a wide grin and played with the scab on his arm. Rudy is quiet and serious, but AJ is a real daredevil. I've never seen anyone with so many cuts and bruises.

Our trainers made squelching sounds as we walked into the scrapyard. There was a huge pile of trash: spare tyres, old mattresses, broken toys, couches, you name it. Beyond that, the yard trailed into a valley where the trees grew wild.

Rudy and AJ raced into the trash, to see what they could find. But, all of a

sudden, I was more interested in the forest. I set off towards the trees. Something was waiting for me there. I just knew it.

I wanted to turn back and call Rudy and AJ, but somehow I couldn't. I felt as though a magnet was pulling me. I walked further into the forest – and tripped over a branch. My skateboard shot ahead and I fell on top of the mannequin.

I got to my feet in a daze and picked up the mannequin. We'd fallen on to a bright green rock. Huh? I looked again, and reached down to touch the rock. The green colour was my fake snot.

Then my hand grew hot and began to throb, like your head does when you have the flu. The rock glimmered and pulsed in time with my hand. I touched it again. The heat and throbbing intensified. Then my hand disappeared into the rock! The heat spread from my hand to my arm and across my whole body. In the distance I could hear AJ shouting. Then his voice faded away as I was sucked into the green abyss.

SSSSHHH

chapter 2

A r r i v a l

It was dark. Pins and needles trickled through my entire body, leaving me dizzy. I fell to my knees. I was still carrying my mannequin and I leant on it for support. My eyes were slowly adjusting to the dark. Suddenly, a huge bellow rang out.

What in the heck was that?

Another bellow. This time it was louder and closer. Panic rushed through my body like a speeding train. The sheer force of the next bellow rocked me forward and I whacked my face against a huge boulder.

The bellows were getting louder and closer. I began to breathe really fast and squeezed my eyes shut. I forced myself to open them again and looked out from behind the rock.

I couldn't tear my eyes away from what I saw, even though it was terrifying. A massive blue, hairy beast lumbered towards my hiding place. It was running its face along the ground. I wondered if it was smelling me out. Every few seconds it let out a loud bellow. The beast would reach me at any moment. I looked over my shoulder. Large rocks were scattered all around. They were big enough to hide behind – if I could just make a run for it when the beast had its head down.

My heart was pounding so loudly that I was scared the beast would hear it. I waited, holding my breath. When it lowered its head, I sprinted to the next rock. I crouched behind it and checked on the beast. It hadn't seen me. I waited again, this time not even aware of my breath. I sprinted to the next rock. I did this six times, until I was safely hidden behind a cluster of rocks, up on a hill.

I could look down on the beast from here – except now there were two! The beasts were huge! They reminded me of the woolly

mammoths we studied in history. White, sharp horns curved upwards from the sides of their heads. They had pig snouts and bucket-like mouths, and long, yellow claws poking out of their shaggy paws.

With each loud vibrating bellow, more hairy beasts arrived. Soon, there was a whole herd of them! One of the beasts raised itself on its hind legs. It swiped at a white bird flying overhead, and smacked the bird into its bucket mouth. I shuddered.

I turned away and leant against the rock, trying to calm myself. The air was hot and hard

to breathe. My hands were shaking and my heart was still trying to leap out of my chest. I felt so tired. I looked upwards. There was only one dim light in the sky. Where was I? Why was it so dark? What were these things?

I definitely didn't want them to be there when I turned around!

I took a deep breath and peeked out with one eye open. One of the bellowing monsters looked in my direction and I quickly pulled my head back. I rolled my hands into fists and felt my nails digging into my palms. I wished AJ and Rudy were with me. I wanted to go home.

My hammering heart froze. How would I get home? Would I see Rudy and AJ again? My family?

The beasts let out a thunderous bellow. My stomach flip-flopped as I looked one of them dead in its red eye. I was sure it could see me. It stared at me for what seemed like for ever, then continued sniffing. I let out a long breath. My leg slackened and my trainer scraped loudly across the gravel. I saw a pebble bounce down towards the beasts. They looked in my direction and bellowed. The ground trembled as they started to gallop towards the hill. They were coming for me!

I sprinted as fast as I could up the hill, dodging the enormous boulders. I didn't know where I was going and I didn't care – as long as it was away from them. My trainer clipped a small rock and I fell to the ground. I struggled to get up but I kept slipping backwards.

I thought my end had come.

I groaned, thinking of the way the beast ate the white bird. Suddenly something cold and clammy clamped around my mouth. I was pulled head first down a dark tunnel.

chapter 3

C a v e   C i t y

I was getting really sick of all this tripping over and being pulled into new places. Nothing positive ever seemed to come of it.

What are you? What do you want?

This question floated into my head like a thought, but it didn't sound like me.

What I assumed were doing the talking – I mean thinking – were the strangest creatures I had ever seen. They looked like little, bald men. They had pale yellow skin, wide eyes, long arms, three fingers with suction cups at the end and big round pot bellies.

A group had crowded around me. Oddly, I felt more curious than scared. I looked past them and saw I was in a massive cave. More yellow creatures stared down at me from rooms carved out of the walls. Hanging from the ceiling were lumpy, multicoloured disco balls that gave off a dim light.

My eyes were sore. I was so tired.

Suddenly, a huge number of voices exploded in my mind. A group of yellow creatures jumped

down from their cave dens. They ran towards me, their bulging bellies glowing purple.

Panic surged through my body. The voices got louder. They were shouting at me. I had to get out of there!

I sprinted to the other side of the cave, looking wildly for the tunnel they had dragged me down. Nothing. Nothing but bare stone walls.

A few dozen yellow creatures jumped from their dens, landing behind me. I was surrounded. I tried to look for an escape route, but my head was hurting badly. How could I stop the voices?

All of a sudden I felt faint. I grabbed my forehead and fell to the floor.

Cold, clammy fingers were on my neck, pushing me down. I struggled. I kicked and punched but I was too tired. More sticky hands grabbed me. Something was being shoved in my mouth. I clamped my lips shut.

One creature fell from the ceiling and jumped on my stomach. I gasped, swallowing

YARGH!

the thing that was being forced into my mouth! I grabbed the creature and threw it against the wall. The remaining creatures backed away. The shouting stopped. So did the pounding in my head. I felt awake again. Before I knew it, the creature pounced on me again, grabbing my hair with its long arms.

STOP IT! A yellow creature pushed through the crowd.

The creatures scattered and the brute on top of me let go of my hair. Its belly turned a deep purple. *The intruder is dumb, Z-kee.*

Now the belly of Z-kee, the creature who had saved me, glowed a pale purple. *The creature is not dumb, R-cher. I heard him think. There is no reason to attack him.* Z-kee's belly faded again.

A bright yellow creature came forward. Its belly turned pale purple as its thoughts entered my mind. *We didn't attack him. Only R-cher did! We wanted to give him a bejais. I heard him think, too. He said he was tired.*

My head felt better. The voices were clearer. These creatures could read minds. And I could read theirs. But what in the heck was a bejais?

I will show you what a bejais is and answer any questions you have, Z-kee interrupted my thoughts.

We can read the minds of intelligent beings only. We can channel thoughts to a group, or to one being at a time – but that takes practice and skill.

"Where am I? What are those blue bellowing things? Who are you?" I asked.

You are in Halycrus. I am Z-kee, this is R-cher and the brighter one is T-kwinia. Those things that attacked you are mountain swine and—

The intruder must answer our questions before we answer his! R-cher interrupted.

R-cher's eyes were narrow and his posture was aggressive. The other Halycrusians had their hands clasped on their bellies and their elbows flopped by their sides. R-cher's arms stretched in front of him, his suction fingers spread out on the floor. A tuft of my black hair lay beside him. His eyes became slits and he leant closer to me. He looked mean. Very mean. Oops, I hoped he didn't hear that thought.

How do we know where he is from, what he is, what he wants? R-cher switched his gaze to Z-kee.

Their bellies changed from yellow to purple several times, but I couldn't hear anything. They were having a private conversation.

Send him back where he came from, Z-kee. R-cher glared at me before walking away to the end of the cave. About ten others tailed him.

Z-kee motioned for me to follow him. He shifted a flat, circular stone on the wall, revealing a tunnel that led above ground.

"No way. I'm not taking my chances with those mountain swine," I said.

It's OK, we'll be under one of the rocks. We'll be safe. I want to talk to you without R-cher. This is the tunnel you came down. Z-kee crawled into the tunnel. I had no choice but to follow him.

Would you like a bejais? Z-kee pressed his suction fingers against the tunnel wall for a few moments. Then an amazing thing happened. The stone wall moved. The once flat wall now had a mound like an air pocket where Z-kee had pulled at it. He plucked a marble-sized orange jewel out of the wall and handed it to me.

This is what they gave you before, to make you feel better. You eat it.

I lightly squeezed the bejais between my fingers. It was soft, like chewed-up gum. I shrugged and popped it in my mouth. It began to grow bigger and bigger and, just when I thought it wouldn't be able to fit, it exploded. Nothing was left in my mouth but a tingling feeling and a really bad, sour taste. Gross.

So, how did you arrive on Halycrus? The way Z-kee looked at me reminded me of my dad, even though he was only as tall as my nine-year-old brothers.

"I'm not sure. I just sort of landed here," I began. But why speak aloud? I decided to think my story rather than speak it. I told Z-kee what happened in the scrapyard.

A mountain swine bellowed in the distance. My heart started to pound again.

chapter 4

Z - k e e ' s S t o r y

Now it was time for Z-kee's story. He clasped his hands on his belly. *Legend has it that our sun has been dying for much, much longer than anyone can remember. All that is left is a white spot.*

I thought of the dim white light I had seen – before I fell flat on my face with the mountain swine galloping up the hill behind me.

Yes, that is our sun. Z-kee heard my thoughts again. This would take a lot of practice!

The tunnel walls shuddered and another bellow rang out. Bits of rock crumbled on my head. It felt like the ceiling would cave in! A terrible stench wafted into the tunnel. I gagged.

That's the mountain swine. Z-kee brushed the dust from his arms. *It is said that long, long ago they lived in the upper ice mountains. But then our planet grew hotter, and they came down to this part of Halycrus. They started to hunt us, so we moved underground. We try to think with them but they're mindless creatures and don't understand. They just search for food. They hunt the white sea birds sometimes.*

I remembered the bird I'd seen the mountain swine eat and I shuddered.

The walls trembled again.

They are vicious creatures. Those rocks you were hiding behind…

I felt embarrassed. The Halycrusians must have seen me cowering like a baby. No wonder R-cher thought I was dumb. The jerk.

Z-kee placed his hand on my shoulder and its clamminess turned warm. *Don't worry. The swine are terrifying. That's why we made this underground city.*

Wow! You made this cave city? Awesome! Did you make it by moving the stone, like you did just now?

Yes, our ancestors made it. Our city is made from the same type of rocks you saw above ground. We get the bejais from them too.

I screwed up my nose. I could still taste the bejais.

A small crack appeared on the tunnel wall behind Z-kee.

The bejais has great power. It is our only food, and when joined together it gives off light.

I thought of the disco balls hanging from the ceiling in the cave city.

Z-kee gave a slight nod. *Yes, but that light is very dim. The bejais down here are not as good as the ones above ground, but we can't collect them because of the mountain swine. Many Halycrusians have died trying. We are trapped. R-cher and his friends sometimes go up, against my wishes, but his disobedience paid off today. He was the one who grabbed you and brought you down to our city before the mountain swine attacked.*

I had thought R-cher was a jerk before? I took that back. What a good guy.

They were using you as a distraction while they collected bejais. They threw the pebble that made the mountain swine notice you.

I reverted to my jerk comment.

R-cher has his own ideas about things, but he is thinking ahead. We cannot take any more bejais from our city. It will collapse if we move the stone around much more.

Dust fell on our heads again. Another bellow shook the tunnel walls.

I have an idea! I'll bring you hammers and chisels. Those are tools on my homeland. You can use them to break off chunks of the rock above ground and then bring them down here to collect the bejais. You'll be much safer!

I started to get excited. That would be an adventure, sneaking out, dodging mountain swine, helping the Halycrusians survive.

Heck, if R-cher could dodge them, I could as well!

But you have to go back to your home to get them. Do you know how to get back home?

No, I didn't. I couldn't help the Halycrusians to collect bejais if I couldn't get back home. How could I keep travelling back and forth between Earth and Halycrus if I didn't even know how I had travelled in the first place?

The tunnel shook violently and a large crack appeared in the walls. A large blue hairy hoof smashed through the ceiling. Stone and dust filled the tunnel. The swine bellowed, trying to get its hoof out. More rocks fell. A yellow claw narrowly missed my head.

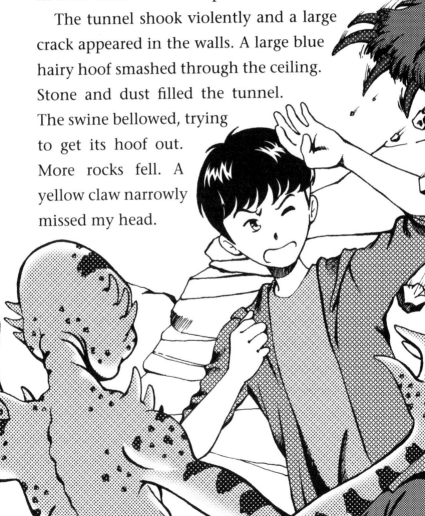

RUN! Z-kee somersaulted down the tunnel towards the city. Coughing and spluttering, I tumbled after him.

Quick, we must seal this entrance before the swine charge through our city.

Z-kee grabbed the large flat stone and blocked the tunnel. Several Halycrusians grabbed rocks to press against the wall.

It won't close. Something is stuck behind it. Z-kee pulled the stone away from the wall.

No! It could be a mountain swine! I picked up T-kwinia's concerned thoughts.

Z-kee reached behind the stone and pulled out my mannequin. He firmly blocked the tunnel entrance. The swine's bellows faded and the ground stopped trembling.

My science project! I picked up the mannequin. It looked as snotty as ever.

Did you say that you were carrying this when you fell? Z-kee asked. When I nodded, he went on, *And you were carrying it when you arrived here. This is how you can travel between your homeland and Halycrus! You can go back home now.*

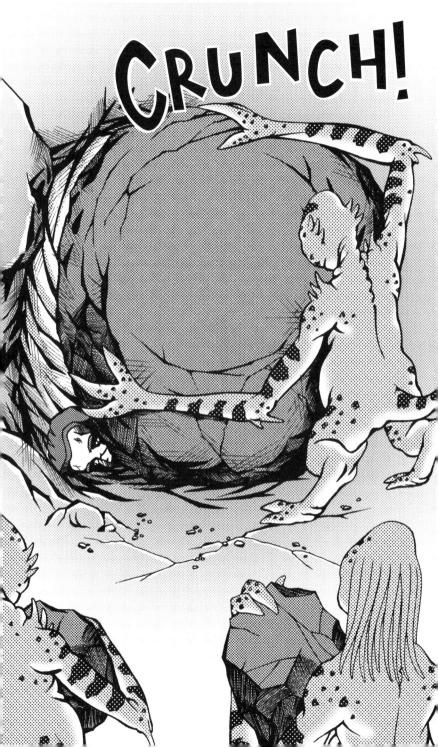

But what do I do? I asked, holding my mannequin by its hair.

Exactly what you did before.

I don't really remember what I did. I told you I just landed here.

Maybe you should close your eyes.

I closed my eyes. Nothing happened. I opened one eye to see Z-kee staring up at me. I closed my eye and willed myself to return home. I felt stupid. Everyone was watching.

Nothing's happening. I felt hot before. I feel warm now but not in the same way.

What's on the face? Z-kee reached out to touch the green slime on the mannequin's face. I explained about snot.

I don't think it's the mannequin that is the link. Smash the face on the ground.

Sure, better the mannequin than me! I raised the head above my own and heaved it on to the rock. The rock began to pulsate and glow green, just like in the scrapyard.

Good luck, my friend. Z-kee squeezed my shoulder. *I'll be waiting for you.*

chapter 5

Back Home

Splat!

I was flat on my back, looking up into the dark sky. The air was cold and I shivered as I gazed through the forest. I was back home.

Pins and needles were still flowing through my body as I slowly walked home. Was I right to promise Z-kee I could help him? I didn't have enough hammers and chisels for all of them! Should I tell my dad? He might be able to get some. But I didn't know if he'd believe me and what if—

"SCOTT! It's eight o'clock! Where have you been?" Mum stood in our doorway, my little brother and sister peeking around her legs.

"Oh – I – um – I was with – um – I was with Rudy and AJ," I finished lamely, ducking into the hallway.

"No, he wasn't!" Penny yelled out from the kitchen. "I saw Rudy and AJ two hours ago and you were not with them!"

Mum ignored her.

"You look sick, Scotty," Mum said. Her tone had changed from angry to worried. "Go to bed. I'll bring your dinner up."

"Psst!"

A stone hit the window when I entered my bedroom. I knew it must be Rudy and AJ. I opened the window and glanced down at two worried faces in the garden.

"Climb up the trellis, but be quiet. Mum thinks I'm sick."

"Where have you been?" AJ was in my room before I had time to turn on the light. Rudy struggled to climb the trellis underneath my window. He paused at the top to take a long puff on his asthma inhaler.

"We waited at the yard for two hours! We were calling out for you but all we found was your board in the middle of the valley! We thought we had to call the police! We saw Penny but I don't think she saw us!" AJ sounded hysterical

but I could tell he was just energised. I knew he was expecting an exciting story. I waited for Rudy to climb into the room before I told them about Halycrus.

"So, what are you going to do?" asked AJ as soon as I finished.

"I'm not too sure. My plan is—"

"Scott? I can hear voices in there. I knew you weren't sick!" Penny's voice floated up the stairs.

"You'd better go, guys. Penny's on the rampage."

AJ rolled his eyes and almost jumped out of the window.

I quickly shut the window after them and turned off the light and jumped into bed. Penny peeked into my room but I pretended to be asleep. A million thoughts were racing through my mind.

✪ ✪ ✪

If I was going to help the Halycrusians collect bejais, I needed lots of hammers, chisels and buckets. Luckily Dad's courier service had recently botched a hardware shop delivery. We had a crate of buckets in our garage. But I only had the hammer and chisel from my tool chest. I needed more. I asked the guys to find whatever they could.

"I've got heaps of old hammers and chisels from woodwork class," said Rudy, arriving at my house with armloads of tools. "The school bought new ones, so these were being thrown away."

"I could only find one hammer." AJ's eyes were wide with excitement.

Rudy cocked his head to the side. "What happens if they don't know how to use them? What if you have to do it all?"

"Who cares?" AJ jumped in. "Scotty's their hero! He's saving their world! Worry about that stuff later. So, can you take all this with you?"

"As long as I'm holding the stuff, I think so. I took the mannequin."

"Are you going to take the mannequin again? That R-cher dude is going to think you have a thing for dolls," AJ laughed.

"I'll just have to prove to him that I don't!" I held up two small foil packets. "I scraped the leftover mixture from its nostrils. It's just enough. One to get into Halycrus and one to get back home. All I have to do is smash it on a rock."

"I wish we were coming," said AJ.

"I know. Me too. But I should go alone. R-cher doesn't like me. Let me get him to trust me before I bring more 'intruders'."

I packed up the hammers and chisels into my backpack and shoved a packet of crisps and a couple of soft drink cans on top. I wasn't keen to try the bejais again. Yuck! I grabbed a stack of buckets and hoisted up the backpack.

"Bye, Mum, I'm going to AJ's!" I yelled towards the lounge. The three of us headed to the scrapyard.

chapter 6

The Plan

I stared into the soulless, red eyes of a mountain swine. This was not a good way to be greeted. The swine looked enormous from fifty metres up a hill – but at eye level? It was heart attack stuff!

The mountain swine was sniffing the ground right in front of me. I was too afraid to breathe. I also didn't want to breathe in deeply for an entirely different reason. Pee-yew! The swine stank! It brought its nose up from the ground and bellowed loudly. Yuck! Its breath was gross too!

Drops of sweat rolled down my forehead. I was a goner. It was centimetres from my face. But it just kept sniffing. Couldn't it see me? Couldn't

it smell me? Well, maybe its own stench clogged
its nostrils.

Scott, look to your left. Z-kee's message floated
into my mind. Out of the corner of my eye, I
saw Z-kee crouched behind a rock. I slowly made
my way over to him, keeping one eye on the
mountain swine. It suddenly turned around. I
froze. The swine looked me right in the eye again
– and did nothing.

Hurry! I have the entry open. Just jump in! I heard
Z-kee shuffle and saw a flash of yellow as he lifted
a flat, circular stone. The swine cocked its snout
towards Z-kee and bellowed loudly. It scraped at
the ground, ready to charge.

Watch out! I leapt in front of the swine, pushing Z-kee and myself down the tunnel.

The ground shook and the swine's snout almost touched our feet. Its stench followed us as we tumbled down the tunnel and the entry slammed shut behind us.

I see the intruder has angered the mountain swine again. R-cher's dark thoughts slammed into my brain.

You have angered the mountain swine many times, R-cher, Z-kee commented. *It was me who angered the swine this time, not Scott. It didn't even notice him.*

That's right. It looked right through me as if I was invisible! I was beginning to resent R-cher's pet name for me.

What about when we found him? He had a whole herd after him! He wasn't so invisible then. R-cher crawled over to me. His group of friends gathered closer and stared steadily at both Z-kee and me.

I pulled myself up and stared right back at them. Z-kee was still, his hands clasped on his belly.

Actually, R-cher, the swine have terrible senses of sight and smell. I believe that when you threw the pebble to get the swine's attention they looked up and saw you. We stand out with our yellow skin. It is hard to see Scott above ground. He looks so different from us, darker. He blends in.

For once, having someone point out that I looked different made me feel special, not weird. Especially since it was Z-kee, sticking up for me.

Now, Scott, tell them your plan to collect the bejais from above, Z-kee continued.

R-cher's voice slipped into my mind like an eel as he said to one of his friends, *I hardly trust Z-kee. As if I am going to trust an intruder.* I knew he deliberately didn't hide this thought from me.

Well, I have eight hammers and eight chisels. All the Halycrusians stared expectantly in my direction. *So I can only take seven others above ground to chip away at the bejais rocks.*

How do you expect us to use things we have never seen before with swine running around? R-cher narrowed his eyes. Muffled sounds entered my head as several bellies turned purple. They sounded like murmurs of agreement.

He can teach us! A pale purple belly lit up in a low den at the back of the cave city.

It was T-kwinia. I was grateful that she answered for me.

I picked up a hammer and chisel to explain how to use the tools.

You just put the pointed end of this, the chisel, on the rock. You then use the flat end of this, the hammer, to tap hard on the end of the chisel several times. A bit of the rock should fall off and you put it in the bucket. Keep doing it until the bucket is full. Then take it down the tunnel. You can then extract the bejais down here. Only the quickest can come.

I can do it. I am fast! T-kwinia answered.

You? R-cher's thoughts sounded mocking. *They'd spot you straight away.*

T-kwinia is very fast. But I think you should only take three, Scott. Z-kee motioned for T-kwinia to come down from her den and then looked towards R-cher's huddled gang. *Q-ster, go with them. I suppose you want to be the third, R-cher.*

I gave all three a hammer, chisel and bucket each. *OK, when we go out we need to stick together and close—*

R-cher cut my thought off. *Q-ster and I will take the hills. T-kwinia, you just stay in the tunnel and hold the entrance open.*

No way. T-kwinia stared defiantly at R-cher. *I'm going above ground. Scott's right. We need to stick near the entrances as Scott said, just in case the swine charge us.*

Q-ster's and R-cher's bellies glowed a dark purple, blocking T-kwinia and me from their conversation.

T-kwinia's thought floated in my head: *We'll just stick together. I don't know what they're up to but I know they won't listen to you.*

I followed R-cher, Q-ster and T-kwinia up the tunnel to put our plan into action. Somehow, I knew we would not be coming back down together.

chapter 7

The Battle

R-cher and Q-ster rushed ahead. I didn't see where they went.

Let's go over there. T-kwinia motioned to a large cluster of rocks. *We have an entrance by that third rock.*

T-kwinia and I began quietly chipping away at the rock. I stared at the bit I'd chipped off. The bejais sparkled pink, blue and green. I wondered if they all tasted different.

I heard faint bellowing in the distance. The chisel was slippery in my hand. I wiped the sweat from my brow, looking around for Q-ster and R-cher. I had a bad feeling in my guts. And not two-week-old-pizza kind of bad. More

like the feeling when you watch something fall but can't catch it.

You'd better stand behind the rock, not next to me. I moved T-kwinia's bucket away from the bellowing. I chipped away at the rock. Every couple of seconds I looked over my shoulder. T-kwinia's bucket was three-quarters full. Mine had only one chunk in it.

A huge bellow rang out and the ground shuddered. The swine were charging!

Go down! I pushed T-kwinia towards the entrance tunnel.

Aren't you coming? T-kwinia paused before lifting the entrance open.

No, I have to see what's going on. I shoved the buckets at her.

I stared around me, and saw a streak of yellow weaving in between the rocks high on the hill. It was Q-ster! A swine was trailing him, swiping at him with its long claws. R-cher was behind them, struggling to drag his bejais bucket down the hill.

You silly human! R-cher's thought sliced through my mind like a sharp knife. *The bucket is too heavy. You told us to fill it up! We can't move it now!*

The swine scratched Q-ster's right leg just as he leapt for an entrance tunnel. The swine skidded into a rock. R-cher was behind it still trying to carry the bucket.

Get down the tunnel, R-cher!

I'm not leaving this behind. This is what we came up to get!

R-cher's yellow arms attracted the mountain swine's attention. It pawed the ground, ready to charge. I sprinted to R-cher, grabbed one of his long limbs and dragged him towards the tunnel. I picked up the flat circle of stone and threw R-cher inside. Before hurtling down after him, I thought I saw another flash of bright yellow on the hill.

Q-ster lay on the cave floor, surrounded by worried-looking Halycrusians. Thin purple liquid trickled down his leg.

R-cher glared menacingly at me. *He is bleeding and it's your fault! The stupid bucket you gave us was too heavy when we filled it up! Swine almost gored us and we left everything behind! What a waste!*

That's why I told you to stick together, close to the entry tunnels, I answered. *You didn't listen! You and Q-ster went off somewhere by yourselves. If you had done what I told you this wouldn't have happened!*

You would have seen the swine, pushed the bucket down the entry tunnel and jumped in before it even reached you, just like T-kwinia and I did!

And where is T-kwinia? She went back for the bucket that was too heavy to carry! What a great plan! R-cher's sneer echoed through my mind as I remembered the bright yellow flash on the hill.

Oh no! R-cher knew she went back for the bucket but he didn't care! He kept quiet about it until he had the chance to belittle me in front of everyone.

I pushed past him and ran up the tunnel to above ground. I saw a patch of yellow, and a big patch of blue. A huge swine was standing over T-kwinia.

T-kwinia, I'm going to throw a rock at the swine. When it turns around, run towards the entry tunnel and do not look back. OK?

I didn't bother to wait for an answer. I hurled a rock at the swine. It bellowed and raised itself to its hind legs. It turned around but was distracted by the bright streak of T-kwinia darting down

GEP

the hill. T-kwinia was a fast runner! She looked like a big yellow rabbit, her long limbs stretching in front and pulling her short body forward.

I dashed towards the swine, throwing another rock. I took a flying leap on to a bejais rock. I jumped on the swine's back. It bucked wildly but I knew I had to keep my balance. Just ride it like a skateboard, dude, I told myself.

The swine reared, smashing me to the ground. I tried to get up but something was holding me back. My backpack was stuck under a bejais rock! I quickly wriggled out of the shoulder straps – just before the swine lunged. It gored the backpack, ripping it open. Everything fell out: tools, crisps, soft drink and my portal packet. I willed the swine to ignore the shiny

foil. It was my only way home! Was it worth the risk to run down and grab the packet?

The swine pierced a can of soft drink with its yellow claw, spraying the fizz in its face. I heard a sizzling noise. Several chunks of blue hair dropped off, leaving a black mark on its face. The soft drink had burned it! I sprinted towards my backpack and grabbed the second can. The swine bellowed, scraping the ground. I

shook the can hard and pulled the ring, flicking the fizzing drink over its ugly, hairy body. With each sizzle, more blue hair dropped off. The swine bellowed and charged away.

I quickly wrapped the tools and portal packet in the ripped backpack, tucked the bucket of bejais under my arm and sprinted towards the entrance tunnel. I threw myself down, landing in a crowd of Halycrusians. They had all been watching.

There was silence for a few minutes while I caught my breath. Suddenly, a thunderous beat filled the cave. *They are clapping me,* I thought.

We are. Z-kee's warm hand was on my shoulder. *That was fantastic.*

You saved me! T-kwinia touched my elbow. (I guess this was as high as she could reach.)

He almost killed you! R-cher's thought cut through the applause and Z-kee's praise.

Lighten up, R-cher. Z-kee touched his shoulder. *He battled the mountain swine! He saved T-kwinia. He saved us! He even saved the bejais!*

R-cher slowly nodded. My heart started to pound again but it wasn't from fear or dread. It was from excitement and hope. There was still so much to do on Halycrus, and I was looking forward to doing it.

Z-kee handed me a pink bejais and I popped it into my mouth. And you know what? It tasted pretty good!

Portal to Halycrus

Portalopedia

Bejais The Halycrusians' only food. It is found in rocks.

Channel To send thoughts into the mind of another being.

Gored Means of attack used by the mountain swine, involving piercing with their sharp horns or claws. Very painful!

Halycrus An alternative world.

Halycrusians Inhabitants of Halycrus.

Mannequin Model of the human figure.

Mind-reading The ability to read another being's thoughts. This is a very handy skill if you cannot understand someone's language, because the thoughts do not need a language.

Mountain swine A massive blue hairy creature from Halycrus. Dangerous.

Portal to Halycrus

Portalopedia

Portal An opening into an alternative world.

Portal mixture A mixture of materials, which opens portals into alternative worlds.

Portal packet A small aluminium foil packet of portal mixture.

Red Sox The Boston Red Sox, a US baseball team.

Upper ice mountains High mountains, which long ago were covered in ice. Once home to the mountain swine.

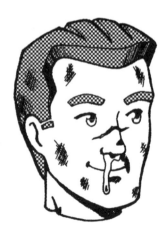